Babies

To Jessie – love auntie Rosbum

For every baby, everywhere – S.W.

First published in 2002 by Macmillan Children's Books
A division of Macmillan Publishers Limited
20 New Wharf Road, London N1 9RR,
Basingstoke and Oxford
Associated companies throughout the world
www.panmacmillan.com

ISBN 0 333 96220 6 HB
ISBN 0 333 96394 6 PB

Text copyright © 2002 Ros Asquith
Illustrations copyright © 2002 Sam Williams

Moral rights asserted

3 5 7 9 8 6 4 2

A CIP catalogue record for this book is available from the British Library,

Printed in Singapore

Babies

ROS ASQUITH

ILLUSTRATED BY SAM WILLIAMS

MACMILLAN CHILDREN'S BOOKS

There are **big** babies
and little **babies**,

do-lots and
do-little babies,

happy babies,
cross babies,

and "I'll show
you who's boss" babies.

There are **bouncy** babies,
funny babies,

and "oh, no,
not the honey!" babies,

wobbly babies, nibbly babies,

and **all** babies are
dribbly babies.

There are babies who
like teddies,

there are babies who
like muddles,

there are babies who
like bathtimes,

there are babies who
like cuddles.

Some babies
sneeze and chuckle,

some babies
squeal and wriggle,

but there's one thing that
all babies love.

If you tickle them, they giggle!

Let's try it: "Tickly wickly wee!"

There are many different babies,
but I'll tell you something true.

The baby that I love the best,
with all my heart, is . . .

YOU!